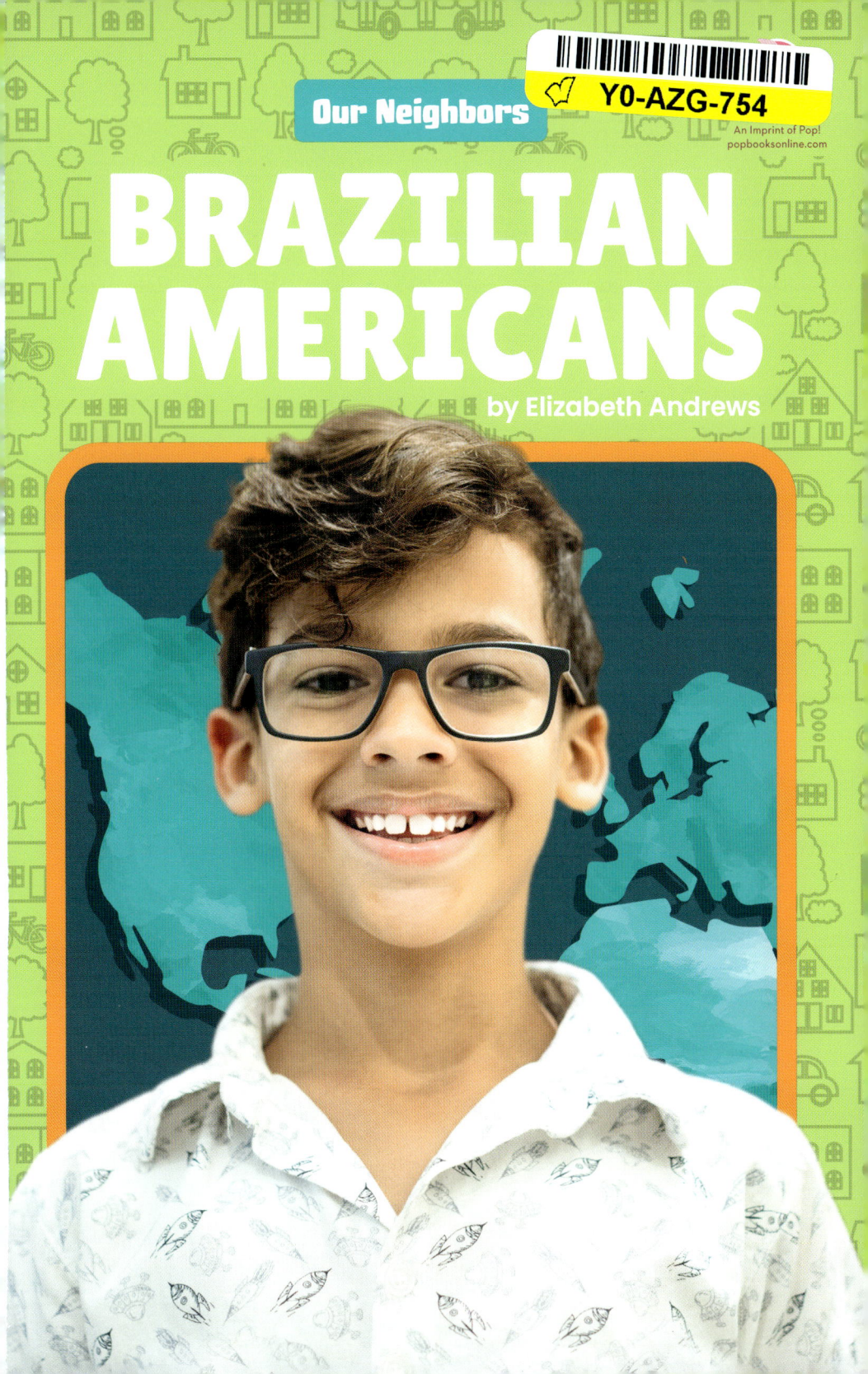

abdobooks.com

Published by Pop!, a division of ABDO, PO Box 398166, Minneapolis, Minnesota 55439. Copyright ©2022 by Abdo Consulting Group, Inc. International copyrights reserved in all countries. No part of this book may be reproduced in any form without written permission from the publisher. DiscoverRoo™ is a trademark and logo of Pop!.

Printed in the United States of America, North Mankato, Minnesota.

052021
092021

THIS BOOK CONTAINS RECYCLED MATERIALS

Cover Photos: iStockphoto; Shutterstock Images
Interior Photos: iStockphoto, 1, 8, 17, 19, 20–21, 25, 26, 27; Shutterstock Images, 5, 6, 11, 12–13, 28; Mauricio Piffer/AP/Shutterstock, 14–15; Gianni Dagli Orti/Shutterstock, 22 (top); Everett/Shutterstock, 22 (bottom); Anonymous/AP/Shutterstock, 23 (top); Sue Cunningham Photographic/Alamy Stock Photo, 23 (bottom)

Editor: Tyler Gieseke
Series Designer: Laura Graphenteen

Library of Congress Control Number: 2020948875
Publisher's Cataloging-in-Publication Data
Names: Andrews, Elizabeth, author.
Title: Brazilian Americans / by Elizabeth Andrews
Description: Minneapolis, Minnesota : Pop!, 2022 | Series: Our neighbors | Includes online resources and index.
Identifiers: ISBN 9781098240011 (lib. bdg.) | ISBN 9781644945957 (pbk.) | ISBN 9781098240936 (ebook)
Subjects: LCSH: Brazilian Americans--Juvenile literature. | Ethnicity--United States--Juvenile literature. | Neighbors--Juvenile literature. | Immigrants--United States--History--Juvenile literature.
Classification: DDC 973.004--dc23

WELCOME TO DiscoverRoo!

Pop open this book and you'll find QR codes loaded with information, so you can learn even more!

Scan this code* and others like it while you read, or visit the website below to make this book pop!

popbooksonline.com/brazilian-americans

*Scanning QR codes requires a web-enabled smart device with a QR code reader app and a camera.

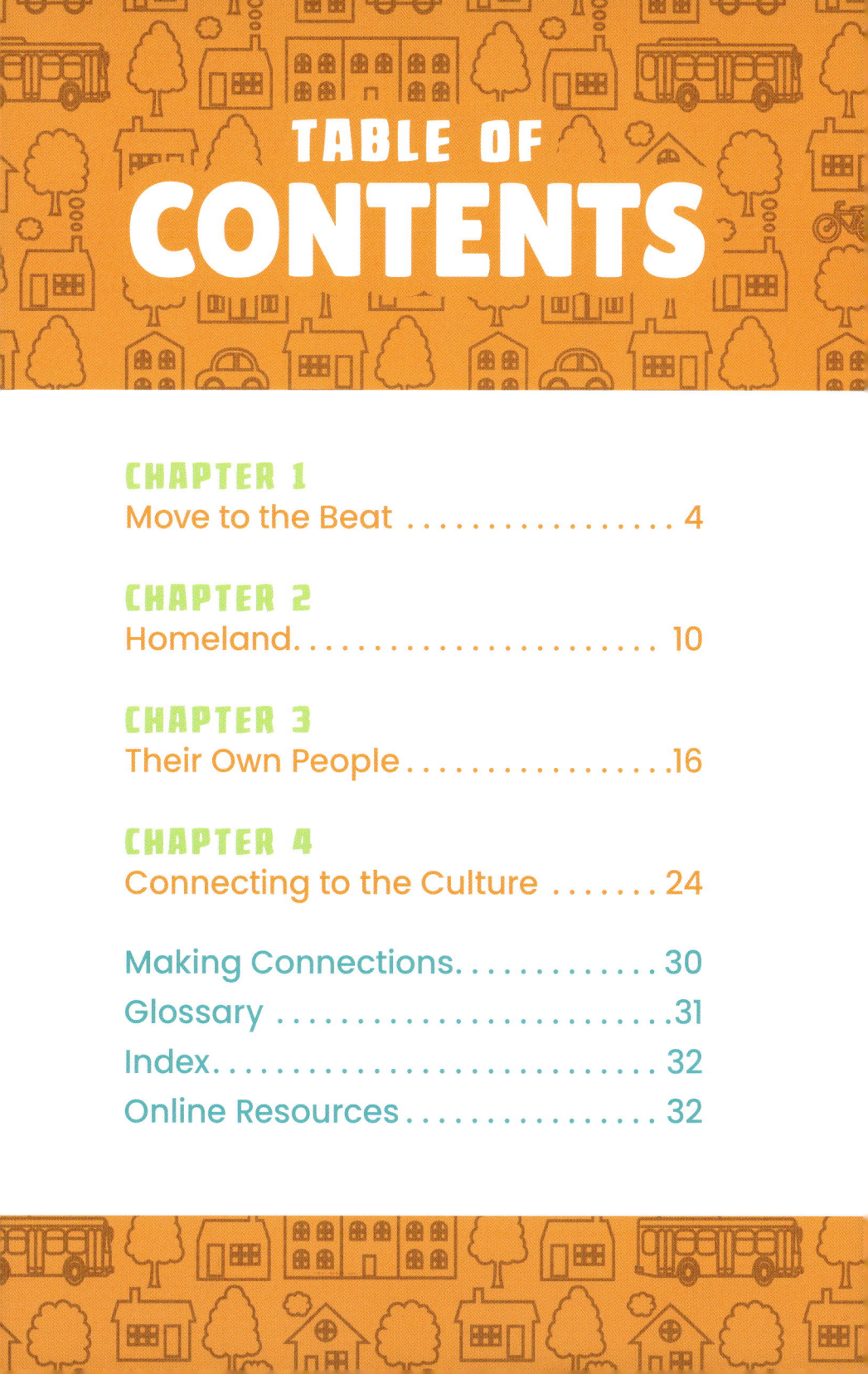

TABLE OF CONTENTS

CHAPTER 1
Move to the Beat 4

CHAPTER 2
Homeland. 10

CHAPTER 3
Their Own People 16

CHAPTER 4
Connecting to the Culture 24

Making Connections. 30
Glossary 31
Index. 32
Online Resources 32

CHAPTER 1

MOVE TO THE BEAT

Enzo takes a deep breath. He looks across the floor toward his partner. She is wearing a feathered yellow dress. They both have numbers pinned to their clothes.

WATCH A VIDEO HERE!

For some Brazilians, ballroom dancing is a life-long activity.

Brazilian samba schools prepare all year to dance in parades.

His left foot taps a steady pattern in his special ballroom shoes. It was the last samba competition of Enzo's ballroom dancing season. He was ready to move through his routine one last time.

Someone presses play on the speakers. A fast-paced song fills the space. Enzo and his partner glide to the beat toward each other. Their hips and arms move smoothly in the same pattern. When they meet in the middle, the spins and slides start.

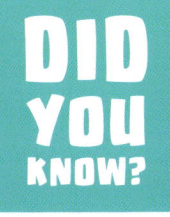
DID YOU KNOW? Samba is a type of dance that mixes African and Brazilian culture.

Dance is a fun way to celebrate family culture!

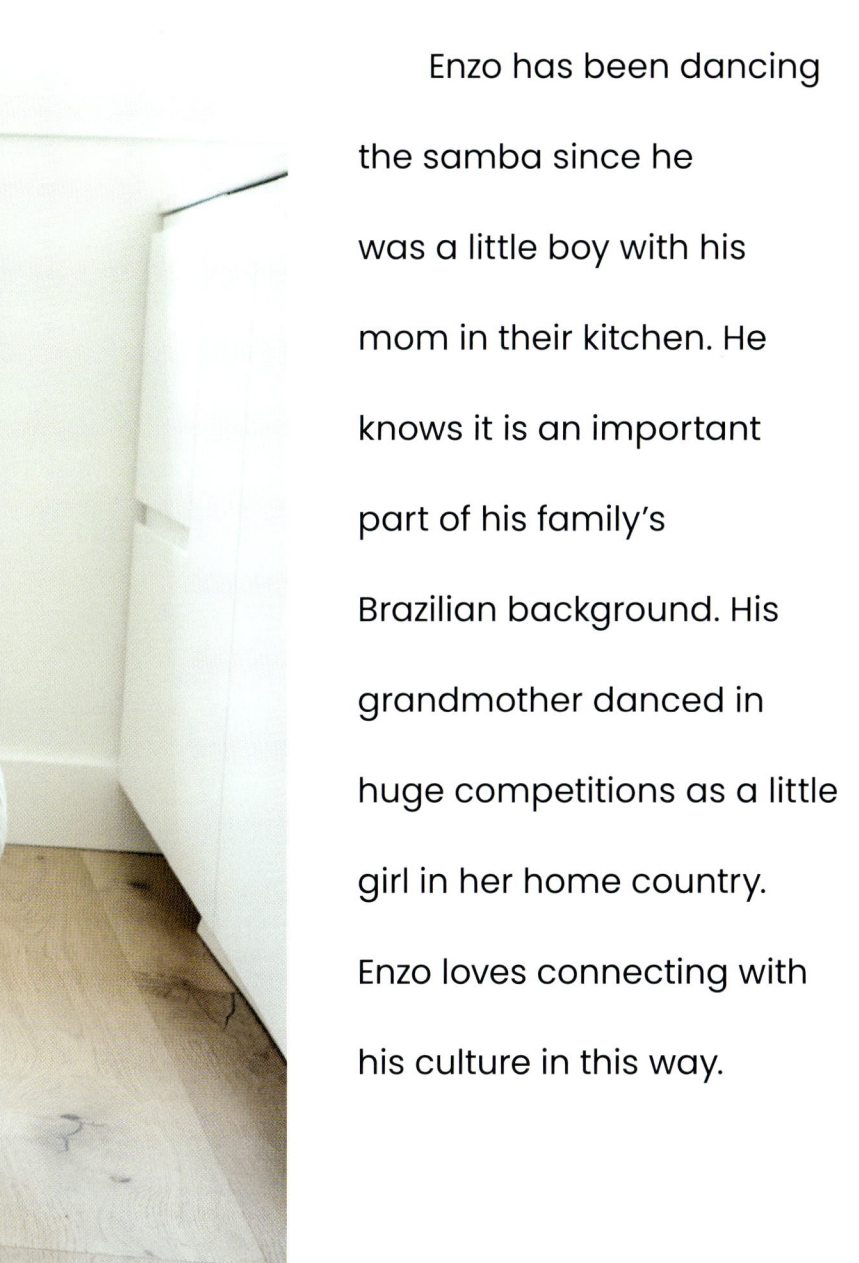

Enzo has been dancing the samba since he was a little boy with his mom in their kitchen. He knows it is an important part of his family's Brazilian background. His grandmother danced in huge competitions as a little girl in her home country. Enzo loves connecting with his culture in this way.

CHAPTER 2
HOMELAND

Brazil is a beautiful South American country. Its people are unique. Theirs is a mix of European, African, and **indigenous cultures**.

LEARN MORE HERE!

DID YOU KNOW? In the late 1980s and 1990s, Brazilians could earn four times as much money in the United States than in Brazil.

Brazil was once controlled by Portugal. In 1822, the country declared its independence. Brazil had a ruling family until 1889. Then citizens started choosing government leaders.

Brazil is home to the Christ the Redeemer statue. It is one of the New Seven Wonders of the World.

Unfortunately, its leaders could never please the whole country. Brazilians were angry and frustrated. In 1964 the military took control. It worked to fix the **economy** and make sure all citizens were safe and happy.

In 1985, the people once again began electing their leaders. They still did not take good care of the country though. Life became very hard and expensive. Many Brazilians decided to **immigrate** to the United States to escape these problems.

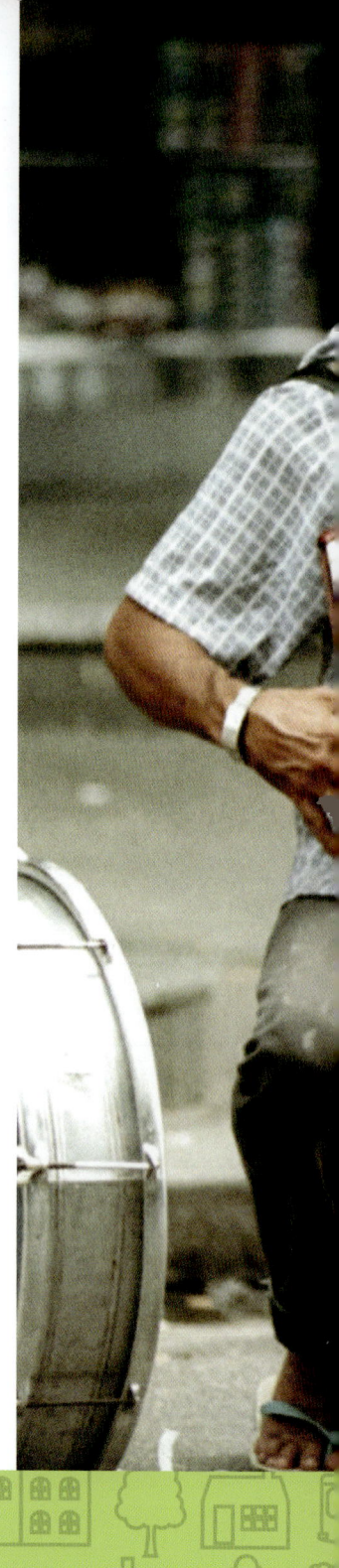

Even during difficult times, Brazilians were able to find joy.

CHAPTER 3

THEIR OWN PEOPLE

Brazilian Americans were not recognized by the United States when they started arriving. They were included in the larger **immigrant** group of Latin Americans. These are usually Spanish speakers from

COMPLETE AN ACTIVITY HERE!

Brazilian Americans can look different from family to family.

Central and South America. This label took away from their **cultural** identity as Brazilian. It wasn't until the 1940s that the United States started recording Brazilians as a separate group.

Children of Brazilian immigrants can feel misunderstood. It's a challenge their parents have faced too. Since they are from South America, their neighbors might assume they speak Spanish. They are actually more likely to speak Portuguese.

Brazil has a colorful **culture** and many special people. When Brazilians

DID YOU KNOW? Brazilians greet each other by giving three kisses on the cheeks.

New York City is home to a big Brazilian American community.

made the move to America, they might have felt lost. This feeling pushed them to move into neighborhoods where other Brazilian immigrants were. Most of them would end up in the northeastern United States.

Brazilians were hopeful when moving to the United States. They loved their home country, but they could achieve much more in America. The parents moved here ready to go after their dreams. They've taught their children to do the same.

Brazilian American parents love to watch their kids grow into strong people.

BRAZILIAN IMMIGRATION TIMELINE

1500s-1888
Europeans enslaved **indigenous** Brazilians and Africans to farm.

1822
Brazil declares its independence from Portugal.

1940
The first recorded Brazilians arrive in the United States.

1964-1974
The military rules Brazil.

1989
President Fernando Collor de Mello tries and fails to fix the **economy**.

1985
President Tancredo Neves dies before his term starts. Later, his vice president struggles to lead.

1990s
Large waves of Brazilians **immigrate** to the United States looking for a better life.

23

CHAPTER 4

CONNECTING TO THE CULTURE

Family is very important to Brazilians. Each member works hard to support one another. When grandparents get too old

LEARN MORE HERE!

Brazilian Americans are always willing to help their families.

to care for themselves, they move in with their children. It is seen as mean to send them anywhere else.

Brazil is famous for its barbecue!

DID YOU KNOW? The most famous Brazilian dessert is a *brigadeiro*. It's made by heating butter, cocoa powder, and sweetened condensed milk together.

Cooking is an activity that brings Brazilian families together. It is also a way they can connect with the **culture** they left behind. Brazil has a lot of coastline. So, seafood is a traditional part of meals. Brazilians mix in European and African **techniques** and flavors.

Paprika, ginger, and coriander are traditional Brazilian spices.

Spending time at church may give Brazilian Americans a sense of community.

Brazilians are most often **Catholic**. It is a religion that is full of traditions. Brazilian Americans sometimes throw big parties for baptisms and fist communions. These are important moments for children. Families want to celebrate them together.

Brazilian Americans are strong and **resilient**. They find strength and identity in their families. They are proud of the **unique** culture they come from. Living in America gives children of **immigrants** the chance of an easier life. They can find their own success.

CARNIVAL

Carnival takes place before Lent in the Catholic calendar. It is a celebration during which people **overindulge** before they must scale back for a few weeks. There are bright, exciting parades to show off samba schools. Music, food, and wild costumes are everywhere you look. Carnival in Rio, Brazil, is known as "The Greatest Show on Earth."

MAKING CONNECTIONS

TEXT-TO-SELF

In the first chapter, Enzo celebrates his family background through dance. What are special ways you celebrate your own family background?

TEXT-TO-TEXT

Have you read other books about immigrants in America? What do they have in common with this title? How are they different?

TEXT-TO-WORLD

Brazilians moved to America looking for a successful life and better jobs. Are there any other immigrant groups who arrived for similar reasons?

GLOSSARY

Catholic — a member of a Catholic church, especially the Roman Catholic Church.

culture — the arts, beliefs, and ways of life of a group of people.

economy — the way a nation produces and uses goods, services, and natural resources.

immigrate — to enter another country to live. A person who immigrates is an immigrant.

indigenous — native to a certain place.

overindulge — to have too much of something.

resilient — recovers from misfortune or change easily.

technique — a method or style in which something is done.

INDEX

Africa, 7, 10–11, 22, 27

Catholic, 28–29

economy, 13–14, 23

Europe, 10–11, 22, 27

family, 9, 18, 20, 24–25, 27–29

food, 26–27, 29

government, 12–14, 23

immigrant, 12, 14, 16–19, 20, 22–23, 29

Portugal, 11, 18, 22

samba, 4–7, 9, 29

Spanish, 11, 18

ONLINE RESOURCES
popbooksonline.com

Scan this code* and others like it while you read, or visit the website below to make this book pop!

popbooksonline.com/brazilian-americans

*Scanning QR codes requires a web-enabled smart device with a QR code reader app and a camera.